W9-ABV-457

The Story of Christmas for Children

Book Design
and Illustration:
Erv Gnat

Ideals Publishing Corporation
Milwaukee, Wisconsin

Copyright © MCMLXXXIV by Ideals Publishing Corporation
All rights reserved. Printed and bound in U.S.A.
Published simultaneously in Canada.

ISBN 0-8249-8075-1

Do you know why
we celebrate Christmas
by giving presents?

We celebrate by giving gifts
To family and friends
To let them know how much
  they're loved
Before the old year ends.

Behind this Christmas custom lies
A true and simple tale
Of how God gave his Son to us
To show his love won't fail.

About two thousand years ago
God sent to dwell on earth
A Savior meant for all mankind;
A maid would give him birth.

His name would be called Jesus
And His destiny would be
To rise from death on Easter morn,
From sin to set us free.

God chose the maiden Mary
To bear the baby boy
Because she dearly loved the Lord
And worshipped him with joy.

One day while Mary was at home,
An angel dressed in white
Appeared to her, and Mary knelt
In wonder at the sight.

The angel said to her, "Fear not!"
And told her of God's plan
To make her mother of His Son
Who'd walk earth as a man.

His words brought joy to Mary's heart
And awe drove out her fear.
Then Joseph, her betrothed, learned
News he rejoiced to hear.

Months passed. Joseph and his wife
Rejoiced each eve and morn
Because the time was drawing near
For God's Son to be born.

Then one day Joseph hurried home
To tell the latest news.
All people had to pay a tax
And they could not refuse.

So Mary packed and off they went
To Joseph's family town.
She rode upon a donkey's back
From sunrise till sundown.

They entered busy Bethlehem
Amid the dust and noise
Of crowded markets: animals,
Men, women, girls, and boys.

Bazaars were filled with fruits and sweets,
Goods heaped on tabletops;
The travelers were too tired to look
As they passed by the shops.

They went from inn to inn and tried
To find a place to stay.
But all the places were filled up
With people who could pay.

Mary, worn from travel,
Was not feeling very strong.
She knew the time till Jesus's birth
Would not be very long.

They found an inn at last
Whose owner said he had some space
Where they could spend the night —
And they were glad to find a place.

The owner led the couple
To his stable in the back.
The animals watched Joseph
While he started to unpack.

First, Joseph turned a manger
Filled with hay into a bed
Where Jesus could stay nice and warm
And rest his sleepy head.

Then Mary on that holy night
Gave birth to God's own Son.
This tiny babe would be the Prince
Of Peace for everyone.

At that same time, outside the town
Some shepherds tended sheep.
While others watched, one played a flute
And lulled his lamb to sleep.

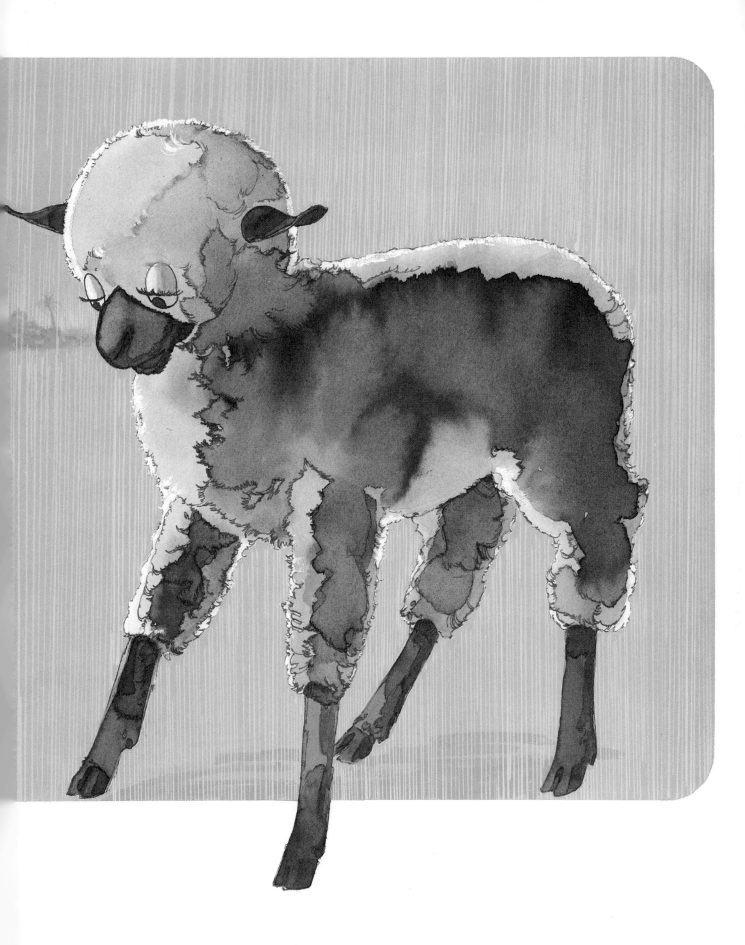

An angel came and said, "I bring
Good tidings of great joy!
Our Savior, Christ the Lord, is here,
A newborn baby boy!"

Then all at once a heavenly host
Of angels filled the sky.
"Glory to God in the highest! Peace
On earth!" rang out their cry.

The shepherds stood in wonder
As the heavens rang with sound.
They started off for Bethlehem
Where they knew He would be found.

Three wise men seeking for the child
Had journeyed from afar
Across the desert sands led by
A brightly shining star.

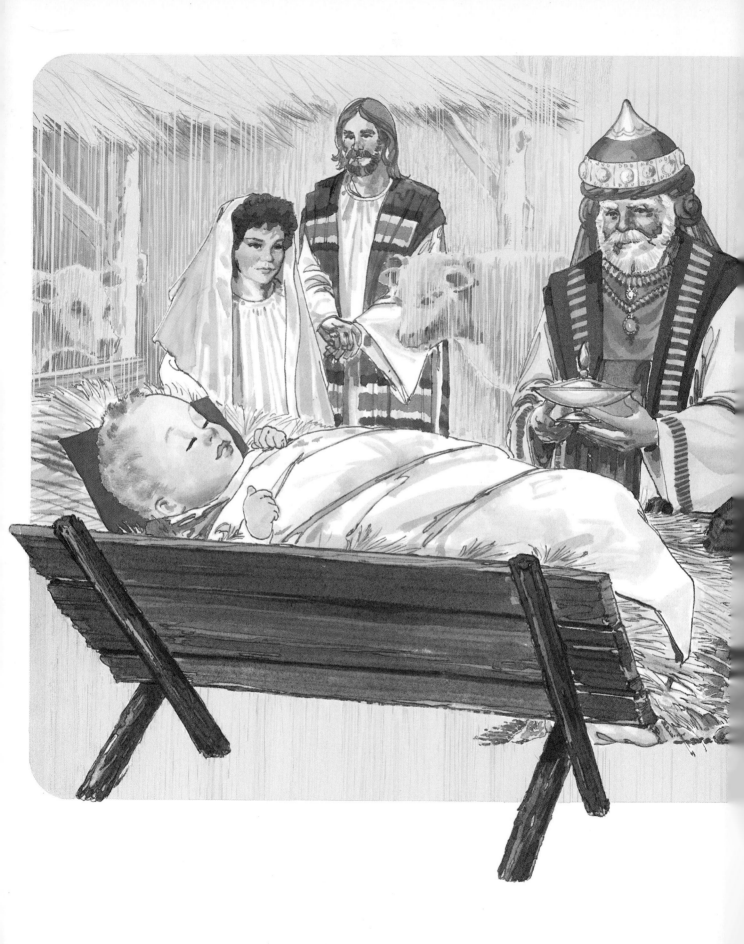

The child God sent to save mankind
Was what the wise men saw.
Their royal gifts joined simple gifts
Placed gently in the straw.

Then each presented Jesus with
A priceless gift of love
In humble thankfulness for this
Best gift from God above.

Inside the tiny stable,
Many people gathered round.
To honor Jesus Christ the Lord,
They knelt down on the ground.

The wise men gave him frankincense,
Sweet myrrh, and brilliant gold.
The shepherds brought him soft sheep's wool
To keep him from the cold.

At Christmas time we give our gifts
Expressing hope and love
As Jesus came to earth for us,
A gift from God above.

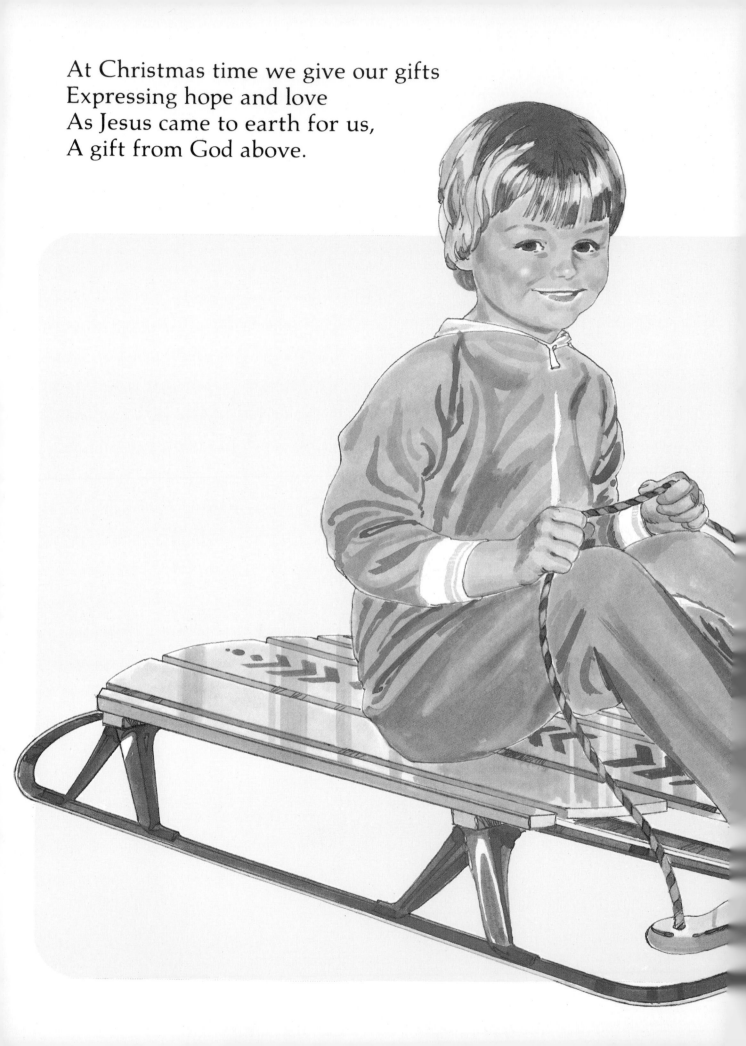

Do not forget the Holy Child
And in his birthday find
A gift for all to celebrate,
The Savior of mankind.

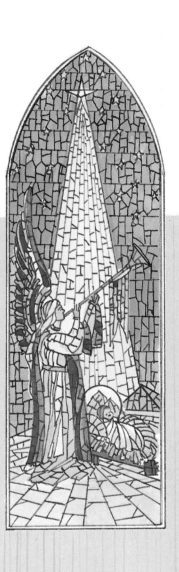

The end

This book belongs to:

Lauren
Spears ♡

I love Jesus